D1410542

THE SOURCES OF THE STORIES

There are many versions of the fairy tales told in this book.
The storytellers listed below wrote, or wrote down,
the best-known versions, on which the present tellings
are based. The date is the original year of publication.

Puss in Boots · Charles Perrault 1697
Toads and Diamonds · Charles Perrault 1697
The Donkey, the Table and the Stick · Joseph Jacobs 1890
The Three Wishes · Joseph Jacobs 1894

This 1986 edition is published by Derrydale Books, distributed by
Crown Publishers, Inc., by arrangement with Walker Books Limited.
Manufactured in Italy

Library of Congress Cataloging in Publication Data
Hayes, Sarah.
Puss in boots; Toads and diamonds; The donkey, the
table, and the stick; The three wishes.
.
(Read me a story)
Summary: Presents four well-known tales from France
and England.
1. Fairy tales. [1. Fairy tales. 2. Folklore]
I. Scott,·David, ill. II. Title. III. Series: Hayes,
Sarah. Read me a story.
PZ8.H333Pu 1986   398.2 [E]   86-8878
ISBN 0-517-61552-5

h g f e d c b a

PUSS IN BOOTS

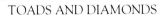

TOADS AND DIAMONDS

THE DONKEY, THE TABLE AND THE STICK

THE THREE WISHES

Retold by Sarah Hayes

Illustrated by David Scott

DERRYDALE BOOKS
NEW YORK

PUSS IN BOOTS

Once upon a time a poor miller died, leaving three sons. To the eldest he gave his mill, to the second his donkey and to the third he gave his cat. 'We're out of luck, Puss,' said the miller's youngest son. 'When winter sets in we shall die of cold. I shall have to make you into a muff!'

Now Puss did not care for the sound of this, and spoke up. 'Do not despair, Master,' he said. 'I can be of great service to you.' The miller's son was surprised to hear his cat speak, but he listened intently to what Puss had to say.

'Just find me a good pair of boots, a hat with a plume and a sack,' said Puss. 'Do as I say and your fortune is made.'

The miller's son did as he was told, and Puss pulled on his boots, set the hat on his head and strode off into the woods. Soon he caught a fine big rabbit in the sack. He strode out of the woods and up the high road to the palace, where he demanded to see the king.

With a low bow and a flourish of his hat, Puss laid the sack before the king. 'Sire, I bring a gift for Your Majesty from my master, the Marquis of Carabas.'

'Your master is most generous,' said the king, wondering who the Marquis of Carabas might be. Of course he could not know that this was just a name Puss had invented for his master.

The next day Puss caught two plump partridges in his sack, which he also presented to the king in the name of the Marquis of Carabas. 'Your master is most generous,' the king said again, even more curious about the mysterious Marquis of Carabas.

Week followed week, and every day Puss
trapped some game and presented it to the king
in the name of the Marquis of Carabas.

By and by Puss discovered that the king was
to take a drive in the country with his beautiful
daughter.

'Quickly, Master,' said Puss. 'Take off all
your clothes and jump into the river. Do as I
say and your fortune is made.' The miller's son
was a little surprised, but he did as he was told,
and Puss hid his ragged clothes under a stone.

As the king's coach passed the river, Puss ran
onto the road, shouting, 'Help! Help! The
Marquis of Carabas is drowning!'

The king recognized Puss, stopped his coach
and sent his men to rescue the marquis. 'Sire, I
must explain,' said Puss. 'Robbers have stolen
my master's clothes and thrown him in the river
to drown.' Immediately the king sent for a
magnificent suit of clothes from his own
wardrobe.

Suitably clad in the king's velvet breeches and a satin cloak, the young man looked so handsome (for he was good-looking to start with) that the princess fell quite in love with him.

Puss, meanwhile, strode on ahead to where some peasants were cutting hay. 'When the king comes along,' said Puss, 'you must say that all these fields belong to the Marquis of Carabas, or I'll mince you into little pieces.' The peasants did as they were told, and the king was much impressed.

Puss strode on until he came to a field where more peasants were harvesting corn. 'When the king comes along,' ordered Puss, 'you must say that all the land round here belongs to the Marquis of Carabas, or I'll mince you into little tiny pieces.' The peasants did as they were told, and the king was even more impressed.

By now Puss had reached a mighty castle belonging to the real owner of the land – an ogre. Boldly Puss demanded to see the ogre. 'I have been told,' said Puss, 'that you have the power to transform yourself into the shape of any animal you choose, but I cannot believe it.'

'It's true!' roared the ogre, changing himself
into a lion. Puss was so terrified that he leapt onto the roof. He had forgotten that his boots
would make him clumsy, and he almost fell off.

'I've also been told,' said Puss, quaking with

fear, 'that you can take the shape of a very
small animal such as a rat or a mouse. That I
cannot believe!'

'Easy!' roared the ogre, and the roar turned
to a squeak as he changed himself into a mouse.

Puss immediately pounced on the mouse and ate him up. So that was the end of the ogre.

Puss ordered the ogre's servants to prepare a great banquet, and hurried over the drawbridge just in time to meet the king, the princess and his master.

'Welcome to the castle of the Marquis of Carabas,' said Puss, bowing low and waving his hat with the plume.

'Your master is obviously a man of great importance,' said the king to Puss a little later, over a goblet of wine. And when the banquet was over, he offered his daughter's hand in marriage to the Marquis of Carabas.

So the princess and the poor miller's son

were married and lived happily ever after. Puss gave up hunting, hung up his boots and his hat with the plume, and lived a life of luxury at the palace for many long years.

TOADS AND DIAMONDS

Once upon a time there lived a widow with two
daughters. One was just like her mother – proud,
bad-tempered and ugly. The other took after
her father, and was kind and good-natured.
She was also beautiful and the envy of all
who saw her, especially her ill-tempered
mother and sister.

One day the good girl was sent out to fetch
water. When she arrived at the well, there sat
an old woman dressed in rags. 'Give me some
of that water, my dear,' said the old crone, 'for
I am thirsty.' The girl drew a cup of water from
the well and lifted it to the old woman's lips, so
that she might drink more easily.

'You will be rewarded for your kindness,' said the old woman, who was really a fairy in disguise. 'Every time you speak, jewels and flowers will fall from your lips.'

When the girl returned home, her mother scolded her for taking so long. 'I am sorry, Mother,' she said, and as she spoke two pearls, three roses and a diamond fell from her mouth. The mother was furious at this piece of good fortune and demanded an explanation.

No sooner was the story told and the floor scattered with jewels and flowers than the mother determined that her other daughter should try her luck at the well. The lazy girl did not want to go at all, but her mother insisted. So she snatched up a silver flagon and flounced off.

When she arrived at the well, there sat a richly dressed lady, festooned with silks and furs. 'Give me some of that water, my dear,' said the lady, 'for I am thirsty.' The grumpy girl had been expecting an old crone and rudely replied, 'Get it yourself! This silver flagon is not for your kind.'

'You are not very polite,' said the lady, who was really the fairy in a different guise, 'and you will be punished for your unkindness. Every time you speak, snakes and toads will fall from your lips.'

The lazy girl dawdled home. 'Well, Daughter?' said her mother when eventually she arrived.

'Well, Mother?' replied the girl unpleasantly. As she spoke, two vipers and a toad fell from her mouth. The mother was beside herself with rage.

'This is all your fault!' she shrieked at her beautiful daughter, and drove her into the forest. There she wandered until she was completely lost and exhausted. She sat down and started to cry.

Just then a prince rode by, and when he saw the weeping girl, he stopped.

'Why so sad?' asked the prince.

'My mother has driven me out,' she replied. As she spoke, three pearls, five lilies and a sapphire fell from her mouth. Entranced, the prince set her upon his horse and rode off to his own country, where they were married and lived happily ever after.

As for the rude girl, she became so unpleasant that even her own mother could stand her no more. She sent her into the forest, where the vipers and toads were quite at home.

THE DONKEY,
THE TABLE AND THE STICK

There was once a poor tailor who sent his only son, Jack, out into the world to seek his fortune.

'I'm too poor to keep you,' he said, 'and you're no use to me here.' For Jack, though a good worker, was inclined to be clumsy.

Jack hung his head and left the house. He had not gone far before he bumped into an old woman carrying a bundle of wood. The sticks scattered all over the road, but in no time Jack had gathered them up.

'You seem a hard worker, even if you don't look where you're going,' said the old woman. 'Come away and work for me.'

So Jack served the old woman faithfully for a year and a day. When it was time for him to go, the woman gave him a donkey from her stables.

'This is no ordinary donkey,' said the old woman, and gave its ears a gentle pull. To Jack's astonishment, a cascade of gold and silver coins fell from the donkey's mouth.

'No ordinary donkey indeed,' said Jack, patting the animal. He thanked the old woman and departed, intending to spend the night at an inn on his way home.

The innkeeper was a suspicious fellow, and he inquired whether Jack had enough money to pay for his bed at the inn.

'Why, I could buy your whole inn,' said Jack, and he went into the stables.

Now the innkeeper was inquisitive as well as suspicious, and he watched while Jack pulled the donkey's ears and collected a great pile of gold and silver coins.

The innkeeper's eyes bulged with greed – he wanted that donkey for himself. So in the dead of night, when everyone was asleep, he crept into the stables and exchanged the magic donkey for a very ordinary animal of his own.

When Jack came home the following morning, he found his father not in the best of tempers. 'As poor as ever, I see,' said the tailor, looking at Jack's clothes.

'Not at all, Father,' said Jack. 'This donkey will make my fortune, and yours. You can give up tailoring forever.'

'We shall see,' said his father.

Jack put a bag on the ground, pulled the donkey's ears and waited. The donkey gave a loud 'ee-aw' and nothing happened. 'Just as I expected,' said Jack's father, and he beat his son for telling lies.

Jack was a resourceful boy, and he soon found another job, this time with a master carpenter. He worked hard for a year and a day, and when it was time for him to go, the carpenter gave him a small scratched table from his attic.

'This is no ordinary table,' said the carpenter. Then he whispered to Jack, 'Just say "Table be covered!" in a loud voice.'

'Table be covered!' shouted Jack, and immediately a damask cloth appeared on the table. The cloth was followed by a knife, fork, spoon, plate, goblet and finally a magnificent hot meal fit for a king. 'No ordinary table indeed,' said Jack, and he thanked his master.

On his way home Jack stopped at the same inn as before. The innkeeper was again suspicious and wondered to himself whether Jack had enough money to pay for his food. Instead of the usual dinner, he offered Jack a modest supper of ham and eggs. 'Ham and eggs!' shouted Jack. 'We'll see about that.'

Jack fetched his table, then set it down, saying, 'Table be covered!' in a loud voice. Immediately the table was spread with a hot meal fit for a king, and to follow there was a swan made of spun sugar. The innkeeper's eyes bulged with greed, but he kept quiet. In the dead of night, when everyone was asleep, he crept out and exchanged the magic table for an identical one he had in his barn.

This time when Jack came home to his father, he had a favor to ask. 'Father, have I your permission to marry?' For he had fallen in love with a girl in the town.

'Not unless you can earn enough to feed your wife as well as yourself,' said Jack's father. 'Which I doubt.'

'That I can, Father,' said Jack. He set down the table in front of his father. 'Table be covered!' he ordered, and waited expectantly. The table looked particularly small and scratched, and nothing happened at all.

'Just as I expected,' said Jack's father. 'This boy is mad.'

Again Jack was beaten for telling lies, but he set off even more determined to succeed, now that he had his sweetheart to think of. He was soon taken on by a master chairmaker, and he worked hard for a year and a day. When it was time for him to go, the chairmaker gave him a sack containing a stout stick.

'This is no ordinary stick,' said Jack's master. 'Just say "Out stick and bang 'em!" in a loud voice.' As soon as the words were spoken, the stick flew out of the sack and began to clatter about, looking for something or someone to whack. 'Back, stick!' said the chairmaker, and the stick obediently hopped back into the sack and lay down.

'No ordinary stick indeed,' said Jack, and he thanked his master and went on his way.

Now it came to Jack on the road home that perhaps it was the suspicious innkeeper who had stolen his magic gifts. So this time, when he stayed at the inn, he made a great fuss of the sack, setting it carefully on the bench beside him and never letting it out of his sight.

The innkeeper was consumed with greed and curiosity. 'There must be something truly amazing in that sack,' he said to himself, and again he waited until the dead of night, when everyone was asleep. Then he crept into Jack's room and began to pull the sack from under Jack's pillow.

But Jack was not asleep.
'Out stick and bang 'em!' he
shouted, and immediately
the stick flew out and began
to whack the innkeeper.

'Stop, stop!' screamed the innkeeper. 'I only wanted to peep.' But this wasn't good enough for Jack, and the stick kept on whacking the innkeeper.

'Stop, stop!' screamed the innkeeper again. 'I confess it. I stole your magic donkey.' But this wasn't good enough for Jack, and the stick kept on whacking the innkeeper.

'Stop, stop!' he screamed. 'I confess it. I stole your donkey *and* your magic table. I'll give them back if only you'll take this horrible stick away.'

At last Jack was satisfied. 'Back, stick!' he ordered, and the stick hopped into the sack and lay down. The innkeeper staggered off to find the magic gifts.

So Jack returned home, married his sweetheart and persuaded his father to give up tailoring forever, which improved his temper no end.

THE THREE WISHES

One day a woodman went into the forest to cut
down an old oak tree. No sooner had he lifted
his axe than a fairy appeared and begged him to
spare the tree. Amazed, he put down his axe
and said he would do as she asked.

'You are kinder than you know,' said the
fairy, 'and in return I shall grant your
household three wishes, whatever they may be.'

The woodman trudged home in a daze. He
sat down by the fire and stared into the flames,
thinking hard. Then he remembered that he
had not eaten yet.

'Is supper ready?' he asked his wife.

'Not for an hour or so yet,' she replied.

'Oh no,' groaned the woodman. 'How I wish
I had a good big sausage right now.'

At that very moment a large sausage fell down the chimney.

'What is the meaning of this?' demanded the woman, and the woodman had to tell her the whole story. 'Well, you are a fool!' said the woman when she saw how her husband had wasted his wish. 'I wish that wretched sausage were on the end of your nose!'

At that moment the sausage flew up and stuck fast to the woodman's nose. Neither the woodman nor his wife could pull it away.

'Well, well, you don't look so bad,' said the wife, looking hard at her husband and thinking not to waste their last wish. But the woodman saw the way his wife's mind was running and quickly wished the sausage off his nose before it stuck there forever.

The sausage landed in a dish on the table, and the woodman and his wife ate it for supper there and then. Even though they were no richer than before, the two thought the sausage was the finest they had ever tasted.